ANOTHER ESCAPADE

John Gumbs

Published by John Gumbs
Publishing partner: Paragon Publishing, Rothersthorpe

First published 2024

ISBN 978-1-78792-062-0

Book design, layout and production management by Into Print
www.intoprint.net

+44 (0)1604 832149

Contents

For Heidi, who set me on the road writing

1

CHANGING TO LIGHT

Christmas had only just gone past and the New year was already in its fifth day when I accidentally bumped into Heidi. She looked really marvellous, and her two blue eyes still had the powerful magnetic force. "Hi," she said, when she saw me. How are you doing?"

"Fine!" I answered. "Still trying to figure out certain things." I was now looking at her like I've never done before when we were working together.

"You still have that power to change to light, and transport yourself anywhere? Well, I'm busy reading about the black holes. There could be something interesting there," I told her.

"Sounds rather interesting, but dangerous."

"Space is dangerous, but exciting. How would you like us to go and visit a black hole, and see how it really works. We could find something new."

"Yes, let's do that," she said.

The last time we were in space, we did not stay long.

"I hope you haven't lost your power. That is so very much important if we are going to travel in light."

She smiled and said, "No, I haven't lost it. I keep testing it now and then. Everything is a hundred per cent. What about you? Have you been doing more research?"

"I have, and lots more thinking."

"Thinking about what?" she asked.

"The big bang, of course, and how it all started."

"From what I've read," she said, "it all began about 13 billion years ago. And that's when time and space began. Space started expanding. It hasn't stopped."

"Did someone or something start it?" she asked. "Surely it cannot just start on its own."

"I've always had the feeling that it was started by another force."

"Well, that's interesting," she said, because our bodies are from that first point."

"It should be wrapped up in our memory bank down through the ages."

"That is so, but it is hard to recover."

"We need to find a nice peaceful place where we can concentrate and change the body to light," I said to her.

We both agreed on a certain place, and went there when it was time. Inside light are particles of photons and also electromagnetic waves.

She looked at me puzzled. "So there's *nothing* faster than the speed of light?"

"So far, absolutely nothing."

"How close to the black hole can we get?" she asked.

"We must be careful not to go too close. One can get tugged in from a great distance away. The black hole we are going to visit is a super massive one in the heart of our Milky Way."

"What are they really for, the black holes? And how great

is the gravity around them?"

"Gravity is very strong there. We have to stay well away from being too close. Light can be dragged in as well, and get warped. That mean all the matter is in one small place and very thin."

"This escapade then," she said, "is very dangerous. We don't know how it will end."

I said to her, "We are safe travelling in light. Only when we return to matter, can things go wrong. There are many planets around having the same makeup as our Earth."

"Let's find one and see what's there!"

"Okay! We'll do that."

We held hands and concentrated on where we want to be. Having heard about a planet they had found we concentrated on that. It was a small one with two stars.

Arriving there, we found that it was just like our own planet, only smaller. The plant life was much different. We saw mountains that were high.

After spending some time looking around we changed again to light and were quite a distance away from the black hole.

We came to another planet with a lot of mounds all over the place. Some very long, others high. It was a puzzle for us what these mounds were for.

Examining one of the long ones, we found a strange entrance. It was rigged up with electronic devices. I said to Heidi, "Come look at this!"

She came close by and saw the contraption. We managed somehow to get the outer door open only to find that there were more doors.

A panel of lights was on them.

Heidi said, "This place is securely guarded. What do you think it could be?"

"Some sort of factory or something like that. I can hear the noise of machines."

Heidi reminded me that we could easily change to light and get into the building – "but it is the changing back that can bring us into trouble."

"You're right," I admitted. "We don't know what is inside the building. The sound is like sewing machines."

It was not possible to see what was going on inside, but we got to the second door, and that was progress made. Carefully, we thrashed out a way to get inside. It was risky and dangerous. I would change into light, go in and see what was going on. This had to be done very neatly. Changing to light was no problem at all; it was changed back to physical in a place that was unknown.

The change took place and I was inside the building. Lots of machines busy doing their work.

The reality hit me hard. I was in a building full of robots, and they looked just like ordinary people. It was impossible for me to hide. I stood in plain view of everything that was in the room. I stood there for maybe five minutes when I was approached by one of the robots that wasn't at a machine. The language that was spoken meant nothing to me. The robot spoke again and waited.

I had a plan just to change into light and disappear. But that wasn't going to give me any information about what was going on. I started speaking in my own language to the robot and I was amazed it understood what I had said.

The robot became very friendly when it learned that I was

from Earth. I told it that we were scientists, and that we were exploring the cosmos. I told it about my friend, Heidi, who was outside by the door. It took me around, by the door, and punched in some codes. Heidi was glad to see my face, and surprised to see the robot beside me.

What we didn't know is, that the robot which we thought was a robot, was actually a human being. They all look alike here. We were told that a ship came from the 'proper' planet, and took the robots that were made here back to base. We saw all the operations of the robots. *Robots making robots.*

The place was very large and everything was working perfectly. We had to leave and go out because the ship was coming in to land.

2

ARTIFICIAL STRUCTURE

"We had never seen anything like this before," I said to Heidi. "What do you think? Would they let us on that ship?"

"We shall try," she said, staring at the ship coming in.

As the ship came in to land, we saw clearly all the details. It had three storeys on top, three beneath, and a rim that was turning with many different colours – like a rainbow.

It came in and stood just above the Earth in a circle of lights shining down onto the ground like a cushion pad. The whole thing was spectacular. Underneath and in the middle was an opening with a pure white light all around the opening and down to the ground. The human man took us inside of this opening, and suddenly, we were on the ship where those who were in charge were.

Those who were controlling the ship were just like the one that was with us. They were all humans. The interior of the ship was out of this world. We could see outside as clear as ever.

And the controls and panels were mind-boggling. We were introduced to the two men on the ship. There were many more, but it seemed to us that they were robots doing their work. They knew quite a lot about the Earth and what type of people we were. They showed on the map what part of the Earth we came from. They had been studying Earth for quite some time.

These people weren't really living on a planet. It was something that they did up – an artificial home that surrounded their star. They asked if we wanted to go back with them and see. We immediately said, *"yes."*

It seemed strange to them that we had no transport and they wanted to know how we got here. Straight away, we told them how we did it, but it wasn't anything new to them. Only they thought that Earth people were not that far advanced as yet.

It wasn't long before they started loading up the robots. This operation was really something to look at. When they were finally finished, we heard a strange whining sound, but felt no movement.

On the massive screen, we saw the Earth moving away from us, then we knew the ship had moved away.

These space people were very advanced with transport. They had ships that could change to light and back again. There were many other things we learned on the trip to their home. They learned from us too, quite a lot about the Earth people. We were known to be a planet of people who were always fighting one another.

As we were drawing near, one of the men pointed out their star, and their artificial home that was quite some way off from the star. We had never seen anything like this. It was a massive artificial structure with a vast space to move around. It got its energy, of course, from the star. How they managed to put it together was something beyond the imagination.

We went through a wide opening like an arcade. It was very high and long. Then finally, it came to a place where there were more ships grounded. It is awe inspiring.

Too much to take in. Other people were busy moving here and there. We do not know if they were humans or robots. It was hard to tell.

We got off the ship and saw on either side rows upon rows of what looked like glass cubicles. They told us that it was a transportation system. As we were walking to go to one of the cubicles, I said to Heidi, "I'm planning to steal that ship we just ceme on."

She said to me, "You're *joking!* How are you going to do that?"

"I'm not joking, but it's going to happen I am planning how to do it."

"It's a rather difficult thing to do, but if you pull it off, our people on Earth would be pleased."

"Yes, they'll gain a lot to have such a ship in their possession. This is way in advance of what our Earth knows.

"How on Earth you're going to do this, beats me. It's a very daring plan, hope it works."

Inside the artificial framework, it was really a work of art. How everything was fitted, and the materials that were used. Such you will not find on the Earth. From inside the room, it looked as though you were going to fall out and go flying, but it was really fantastic, a beautiful view all around.

Heidi approached me again, trying to get more information from me about the ship. When we were talking to the pilot, I took in quite a lot of what he was doing. So many panels of different light would send one crazy. I concentrated hard on three sets of buttons. The middle rim of the ship is what makes the whining sound.

"What about the lift?" Heidi asked. "Did you see what happened?"

"I think I did,"I told her. "More than one button was used to get the ship to lift up. I still remember them."

"There's another problem. Robots will be inside the ship, and many more surrounding it," Heidi said.

"How did you know that?"

"I saw how organized they were, and when we got off the ship, quite a number of them started attending to it," she told me.

"Have you seen anything green, like grass or a tree?" I asked, looking puzzled.

"I haven't seen anything like that, but don't forget that this is an artificial place.

I said, "They don't sneeze, cough, spit and cry like we do."

Heidi said, "For Christ sake, they're *robots*, just machines."

"Yes, but the humans are different. It's them I'm referring to."

"They're so kind and hospitable. I don't think that they have any hurt in them."

3

STEALING A SPACESHIP

"What if they find out what we are going to do? What then?"
I said.

"Let's hope your plan goes off without any problem."

"I'll have to be very careful with those robots inside the
ship." I explained to Heidi. "I hope that when I change to
light to get inside the ship, that I would land where no one
notices me."

Heidi said, "That's going to be dangerous, changing back
to normal, you could land anywhere on that ship."

"That's the chance I'll have to take." I told her.

"Before you came up with the plan of stealing the craft,
we were shown many places, met a number of important
officials, and were told quite a number of useful things.
These humans are very technological."

"They are really way in advance of us."

Concentrating deeply and visualizing the place you want
to be is very important when changing to light. I did just that,
and got myself into the craft. Luckily, where I changed back,
there was no one in that area.

On the trip from the planet to the artificial structure, I
hadn't noticed certain things. I was too busy concentrating

on what the pilot was doing.

The interior of the craft was out of this world. Beautifully decorated with what looked like crystals in different colours. I remembered clearly the pilot's area. All the different coloured lights, switches and knobs.

Some of the robots were well away from me, so I had time to get myself in a good position without them seeing me.

I punched a button, just like I saw the pilot did. Then there was a screen, and I was asked for a code. I was stumped. How foolish was I, thinking I could just go and steal a craft! It really wasn't that simple. But then, I saw these letters and numbers on the side of the screen.

I wasted no time in punching them in. I heard the whining sound of the main rim. At that moment, the robots that were on the ship roused themselves from where they were and came closer to the pilot area.

Back in our room where Heidi was, we had already made arrangements that if anything went wrong, what she should do.

I was surrounded by the robots, and was left with only one thing to do. The ship was already tuned for transferring to light, and its destination was Earth.

Two of the robots had me in their grip. Out of the corner of my eye, I saw a light, then a form – it was Heidi. The robots didn't see her.

The ship was now moving out to the entrance of the arcade, and in no time, it was up in space. I found out later, that it was controlled by automatic pilot.

Heidi was spotted by a robot who was now moving to where she was. The robots are all mechanical things and are programmed not to harm. They send back signals to HQ.

Heidi knows quite a lot about computers and robots. As the robot came near to Heidi, she wasted no time, and put it out of control. The robot fell back onto the ground panel. Heidi went and took the cartridge out of the arm below the elbow.

Outside, there were many small crafts around. The two robots that had me in their grip, suddenly let go. Heidi came over, and did what she did to that robot. They just collapsed, and were no more active.

"This escapade is bigger than we thought," Heidi said. "If we get out of this one, we're very lucky."

"These human beings with their robots are not going to harm us. They're only going to protect what is theirs." I said.

"It is still dangerous. Tell me what's going on so far."

"The ship is on automatic pilot. It's been tuned to change to light in a few minutes time. Its destination is the Earth."

"Are you actually saying that we're going to get away with bringing a spaceship to Earth?" Heidi was a bit shocked.

"For many years the people on Earth have been hearing stories about aliens. But nothing really showed up."

"Penetrating our atmosphere with a beam of light, they won't know what's happening," Heidi said, realizing what was taking place. "And we have a few robots as well. No aliens."

"We've ended up with something fantastic. A spaceship. Who is going to believe that? Well, here it is."

"It's going to be the biggest news on Earth. You can bet your life on that!" Heidi said.

Suddenly, we weren't there. Time left us. We could not recall anything until… we saw where we were.

*

The cows in the field were grazing. The ship landed in the middle of a big field. We were back to our normal selves. The small crafts did not land, but stayed high in the air.

Many people were already out and surrounded the ship. In no time, the whole field was packed with spectators.

The main rim came to a standstill, no more whining. We opened the entrance and stared at the crowd.

All along, the small crafts had been tracking us even when the ship changed to light. They were in full view of everyone, and didn't do anything about it. They just stayed where they were.

The main computer knew exactly where Heidi resided, and that's where the ship landed. All the news people were there. More and more people were joining the queue, and there were thousands of people to see the craft.

High officials came along and entered the craft. At that same time, the main computer gave a message:

We are a peaceful people living on an artificial planet with a small star. We are 7 light years from your own planet. Two of your people have taken one of our big ships without permission. We want our ship back.

4

KEEPING OUR SECRET SAFE

I said to Heidi, very softly, "I sense we are going to get into trouble with our own officials. They're going to want to know everything. How did we get to the planet. You know what our people are like!"

Heidi said, "I found it rather strange when you said the idea you had to take the ship away. It is done now, so let's not fuss over it. Of course, they would question how we got to that planet without a ship."

"I admit that it was my fault," I said. "I should have not come up with such a plan. But come to think of it, our people might benefit in some way from it."

Heidi said, "You are lucky too. If those people on that planet were like our people, you would have started a war. They would not take it like those people have done."

"I can see now why no one makes contact with us. They know that we do nothing else but war."

The robots on the ship were taken away for inspection and Heidi and I had to go into an office to make statements.

The ship could not be moved for no one had any

information about how it worked. The main computer had the power to move the ship.

For hours on end, they grilled Heidi and myself wanting to know if we were taken by aliens to their planet. We told them that one day we woke up and found ourselves there. They didn't accept that story.

We were pleased with ourselves for having kept the secret of our travels from the officials.

The whole area where the ship had landed, was now cordoned off. People were now in an ordely queue, so that they could get a peep of what was inside the ship.

Those coming back out of the ship were all amazed with what they saw. And of course, to get into the ship, they had to go underneath where the circle of lights were.

You could see many people were touched by seeing such a spectacular spacecraft – it was really spectacular.

Heidi and I hadn't seen all of the ship – only where the pilot area was.

After investigations were over with the officials, we went and looked over the ship more intensely. The television cameras were rolling away, photographers were busy snapping away. This was a day that will go down in history, and never be forgotten

I was now thinking, how are they going to get the ship to start if there's no pilot? That was something they hadn't thought about.

The small crafts were still hanging around above the ship. They seemed to not be doing anything or couldn't do anything. Then the officials turned and asked Heidi and myself if we could pilot the ship seeing that we came with it.

There was one thing none of us knew about. The officials

and the workers had brought out the robots, but they had forgotten one that had been working on the system of the circle of lights. The robot saw on the screen everything that had happened. The ship landing, and all the people coming and going. This robot was a special one. It had no cartridge in its arm.

A special robot that was programmed to know more than the others.

Most of the technical stuff on the ship was seen to by this robot. If any of the computers failed, it would sort them out.

It must have been a long time down by the circle of lights area when Heidi and I were on the ship. We hadn't seen it around, don't even know what it looks like.

When we had boarded the ship from the planet where they were making the robots, we hadn't thought about looking for a special one. I was too busy looking to see what the pilot was doing. The ship was really too big for us to examine everything that was on the side of it. This special robot could have been anywhere.

Without any sort of warning, the ship started moving upwards, with those who came to visit, still inside. The officials were all baffled for they didn't know what to do.

Even some of the scientists who had come along to see the ship, were racking their brains of what they could do. They were all top scientists, and knew about space and spacecrafts. But this craft was way beyond them.

What did they know about matter changing to light and back again? Or of the three-rim system with its rainbow colours, and the circular lights beneath?

Our scientists knew quite a lot. They were still a long way off understanding the workings of the ship they were now looking at. They had noted down what they had seen.

The crystal workings with the rainbow of lights really had them baffled. They had never seen that before. The elevator system was something that they began to discuss between themselves. This ship was out of this world.

We made up our mind, Heidi and me would look after the ship. We were left with one choice – to change to light and get into the ship. If we did so, our secret would be known, but there was no other way to get into the ship.

People were looking at us strangely, as we suddenly appeared. I told Heidi to stay around in the pilot area while I went down to the area where the circle of lights was.

Reaching the crystal door, I got clearance inside. Then I took the elevator down to the circle of lights. I came out of the elevator only to find three more robots there. I looked around to see if I could find that special one, but it was nowhere to be seen. Immediately, I turned and went back into the elevator to get back up to the pilot area.

People were still on the ship looking around, and being amazed that the ship was up off the ground, and just floating there. I got the ship back on the ground again so that the people in it could get off.

5

DEALING WITH THE
SPECIAL ROBOT

After we had landed, we had a quick chat with the officials. I took the ship up again quite some distance from the ground.

Heidi came and said to me, "That special robot, there's something strange about it!"

"What do you think?" I asked. "Can you dismantle it?"

She said, "It's not like the others with a cartridge. This is a special one. I'll have to find out where its power is coming from."

I said, "I have to go back and search the circle of lights area properly. I didn't do so the first time. The ship at the moment is floating, it will not go anywhere. I'll be back in a while."

I left Heidi again and went back down to the circle of lights. What a technological set up that was. Mind blowing. I went down a few steps, reddish in colour, and then there I was standing by a crystal railing that went all the way around. Below that, there was a curvature, then a cone shaped structure with what looked like slanted panels. A crystal circle right at the bottom.

As I came to the rail, the robot appeared. I pointed to it to follow me up where I came from. This robot didn't know the language of the Earth people. There are so many languages, it would have been out of its range to know them all. So it would have been pointless to try and make conversation.

I got a great shock when the robot spoke to me in my own language. I was wrong thinking that it didn't know our language. It did.

Walking up in front of it, I stopped and told it my name. It said that its name was Apelon. I told it of my friend and what her name was.

Arriving at the pilot's area, Heidi was there, and the robot took her hand.

I said to her, "This is Apelon. It is loaded with information that we could possibly use."

Heidi began with her eyes examining the robot to see if she could find any place where cartridges could be placed. She found none.

Apelon said, "Áll the information that is within me is in my main part. I have no cartridges like the other robots."

I said to Apelon, "We already found that out."

Heidi said, "I think I know what's going on. I've been to a factory here on our planet to see how they make the robots. The only thing that planet we came from have on us is the fact that their robots are just like human beings."

"Our robots are not as smart as these ones."

There was a strange mark on the neck of Apelon. Heidi put her hand out and touched the mark. The robot fell down, and couldn't function anymore.

"MY GOD, WHAT HAVE YOU DONE, HEIDI? WHAT HAVE YOU FOUND?" I cried.

She was amazed. "The robot is out of order!"

We began to inspect the robot and found on its right side, a thin split, going down to the bottom. Carefully, we managed to open up the slit with our fingernails. We now had the robot in two halves.

Straight where the chest was Heidi saw the central processing unit. She took it out. She also took the main memory card. It took us a while before we actually decided to keep the robot. Seeing that it looks just like any human being, it might come in handy.

*

I brought the ship back down just above the ground. Heidi and I had more talks with the officials. Convincing them of what was really going on with the changing of light business wasn't an easy task. They had seen for themselves that we had changed from matter to light.

It was a great scientific secret, and Earth had not yet got to that area.

People were allowed again to visit the ship. Now the ship will stay right where it is. It will not move to any other place. In time, we'll probably send it back to the artificial planet from which it was taken.

The small crafts that were around somehow disappeared from the area. It was getting late now, the sun had already sunk below the horizon. I shut down the system. The visitors started leaving the area.

The following day, early in the morning, there was a long queue. It was impossible to get rid of so many visitors. Inside the ship, I brought the controls into view, set the circle of lights on, with the main screen in operation.

It was very clever how they built their robots. The outer skin looked just like humans. Then there was another, very thin and crystal looking. And there was a third that covered the working parts.

The special robot was now dismantled, and we had all the parts ready to take away. Our plan was to check it out carefully, and then put it back together again. Heidi's understanding of robots was first class.

Putting back the robot together again was an adventure. There were parts that were very easy to put together while some parts gave us a hard time. We finally got it back in one piece, just like it was before. It was now functioning again.

I said, "Hello, Apelon, welcome back!"

Apelon said, "I can hear you, you don't have to shout."

Heidi said, "Apelon, glad you're back. We're going to do some tests with you in connection with the ship and the main computer. Then we'll know that everything is good.

We did all the tests – even the complicated ones – and it was all a hundred per cent.

*

On a certain date, Heidi and I were to report to a committee of six members. It was all about me taking the ship away from the artificial planet, without permission, and also to explain how we got the power to change from matter to light and back.

I knew that they won't let me get away with what I had done – taking the ship from the artificial planet without permission. Heidi knew nothing at all of what I had done, until I told her, and she was shocked that I had done such a thing. There was nothing Heidi could have done. I had already taken the ship away.

The officials weren't at all pleased. I should not have taken the ship which was not my own. And being a native of the Earth, it can cause lots of problems.

I knew that the committee had come to realize that I had the ability to change to light and disappear, so they came to the conclusion that the case would be thrown out because of 'strange scientific' circumstances.

When I heard what they had done, I was glad for I always had the feeling that it won't be easy.

Daily, thousands of visitors came to the ship to have a look at it. The officials were making quite a lot of money from the venture.

Heidi and I got Apelon to the pilot area, and made sure that he was in contact with the main computer. Some strange things came up on the main screen that we knew nothing about.

Step by step, Apelon explained what was going on. The main computer itself showed us quite a lot. We were satisfied with the information that we got.

6

THE MEMORY BANK OF APELON

Visitors saw on the screen pictures that they had never seen before. They were seeing shots from deep space. One of the shots of our own Earth was truly amazing.

Everything so crystal clear. Then there came on the screen strings tied together representing a bridge disappearing into a thick cloud with stars all around.

It was now late in the evening, and no more visitors were left on the ship. This was a chance for Heidi to get into the memory bank of Apelon. It was going to be a complicated business. I nearly burst out laughing when Heid told me that she was going to hypnotize the robot.

"Hypnotize the robot?" I questioned her. "How are you going to do that? Why don't you get inside and get into the memory bank?"

"There's an easy way," she said. "Hypnotize it and get all the dormant memory – the memory that is almost forgotten, but just lying there."

"That's brilliant." I told her. "You are the expert. I'll just watch."

"Don't forget," she said, "it looks like a human being, but it is a robot. It's just a machine."

"I know. I know. Just want to see how you're going to hypnotize it. This is something new to me."

"Instead of taking out the memory card, I'll just get Apelon in a subconscious state, then I can get into the realm of its memory."

Heidi had the robot in one of the crystal chairs, and then she began her work on it. The result was amazing.

While I switched over to the auxiliary screen, Apelon began talking. Suddenly, there were pictures on the screen. We were seeing empty space. Nothing there at all. His people had come from another system and began the building of the artificial planet. They had brought along many crystals and other stuff.

They stumbled accidentally on something that was dark, but was good in keeping things together in space. Quite a lot of information came from Apelon.

Then Heidi brought Apelon back to reality, and all was back to normal.

Information that we got from Apelon told of a neighbouring planet that was very friendly with the people on the artificial planet. They had heard what had happened with the taking away of the spacecraft. Apelon said that they were planning to attack Earth.

After we had shut down the spacecraft, and everything was quiet, I said to Heidi, "I have to inform the officials of what's going to take place. This is really serious stuff."

Heidi said, "See, taking the craft away has brought on an interplanetary war. Earth has no spacecrafts, so how are they going to defend themselves?"

"Maybe I can use this craft. In the light mode, they won't be able to find it, let alone destroy it," I told her.

"If I knew beforehand that you were going to take that craft, I would have stopped you. You only told me that you had a plan."

"It could have gone wrong, I know. But luck was with me."

Heidi said, "Let's see what we can find on the main computer tomorrow. We might be able to get more information on how to defend ourselves."

"You haven't got a pretty face for nothing," I said. "That's a great idea. Tomorrow we'll do just that."

The following day while visitors were still queueing up, we entered the craft. The main computer was switched on, and we set it to battle tactics. We were absolutely amazed with all the information that we saw. It was more than enough.

The enemy uses meteorites as a first attack before they come in with their ships. Luckily, we have our atmosphere that can prevent a direct hit. But the meteorites still get down to the planet.

7

THE INTERPLANETARY WAR

Our fighter planes are no good against spacecrafts, so we cannot use them. One minute a spacecraft is there, and in an instant, it is gone. We have no aircrafts that can manoeuvre like that.

I met up with the officials again and gave them the news about what was going to happen to the Earth. They were all angry with me for bringing all this upon them. They got onto their mobiles and gave the order for a 'red alert'.

Earth was ready for any attack that would come from space. They weren't taking any chances. Preparations were made for defence.

*

A few weeks later, meteorites started falling to the Earth. They were all of different sizes.

I had already taken the spacecraft from where it was, and up into space, away from the area where the meteorites were falling. We could knock some of the meteorites off course with our infrared laser beam.

More and more meteorites fell like falling rain. At this rate we could not do anything. Information came over the main computer that the neighbouring planet Creslotan was preparing quite a number of spacecrafts. The artificial planet does not go to war like all the other planets do – they stay peaceful. They had no plans of attacking Earth because I took one of their crafts away. Help came to them from other places, and they knew what Earth people were like.

The Earth had never had any contact with other human beings or any other species from space. They had done all that they could in order to make contact, but so far, nothing came about.

The nearest they got to was me bringing the spacecraft with those robots. The spacecraft was a treasure to them. Robots were something else. There was nothing special about them. Earth had the ability to make them as well. Heidi was one of the experts and knew about robots inside out. Earth was hoping that one day the robots could be doing the dangerous works that humans do.

Moving to another area in space, we could see the area where the meteorites were falling.

Earth was in much danger.

While Earth was busy and trying to find life in the universe, they had no idea whatsoever that there was a planet in one of the galaxies in the Milky Way that was interested in them. This planet belonged to a solar system which had only four planets around it. The people on this planet were in some ways like the people of Earth – warring against their enemies. Only that they did not fight against each other.

Their technology was way in advance, hundreds of years in front of the Earth. They had all these different types of spacecraft that would have pleased the Earth people to be looking at. There are some old stories about a race of people who had lived on the Earth a long time ago. They had moved up to Mars, and from there, deeper into space.

There must have been some reason why the people on this planet were so interested in the Earth and its people. With a great force gathered, they were coming to rescue the Earth from its enemies.

Heidi showed me on the big screen the type of robots that they had. There was a group of robots who could turn their heads all the way around, and they were programmed to have feelings.

"Feelings!" I was surprised to hear that. "You mean the same feelings that we human beings have?"

"Yes," Heidi said. "These people are way ahead of us. Our main computer says that they are dealing with crystal light."

"Now that is really way beyond Earth people. You mustn't forget that you and I can change to light whenever we want to. But we still do not know a lot about it."

Heidi said, "There's no mass within the photons which has its own wavelength. With crystals, that's different. There are units of microscopic atoms."

I said, "It would be interesting to do some research there!"

The planet that was interested in assisting the Earth against its enemies was called Antera. Antera sent out 150 mother ships each carrying 50 small crafts. Above the Earth were hundreds upon hundreds of spacecrafts, all different shapes and sizes.

The people on Earth had never seen anything like this before. They had, of course, read stories about the past where such things had taken place.

The planet Creslotan had their crafts out as well. They were a reddish-pink. Some of their crafts were the same as what Heidi and I were in.

*

We landed our craft safely to where it was, then we watched as the war between the planetary forces started. Sometimes you'll see a craft, then it would disappear, and then reappear. This went on during the whole confrontation. Quite a number of crafts from the planet Antera had landed, and robots like human beings were helping people. The whole skies above the Earth were covered, and fighting went on.

Creslotan lost many ships while they were in the physical state. One of the strange things that happened, there was no wreckage falling to the ground, it just *disappeared*.

The robots from Creslotan had this special small hand gun that pointed a light on the individual human being, and they were no more. Their inner selves were already taken and recorded on the spaceships. The war carried on with much damage to Creslotan, while Antera had not much damage.

The people on the artificial planet didn't do anything because they had the people from the planet Creslotan helping and protecting them.

We forgot to set the invisible electromagnetic shield around our craft, and it was too late to stop the enemy. They came and overpowered us. We had no time to be concentrating and changing to light...

Placing a strange headgear on our heads, they took us away. A few seconds later, we were in one of their crafts.

*

This mother ship that they brought us to was massive. It was high and very long. The ship we got from the artificial planet was taken back.

Having this strange headgear on blocked our chances to escape. Heidi and I already know what we have to do when we got into situations like this. We have to play it cool, don't make any fuss, and when the right time presents itself, we take it. I must say that they treated us well. They questioned us separately for about one hour. We were then put in separate rooms, but close to each other. When the door slid to the left, there was a thin corridor and a glassy looking partition, but with a clear view into space.

I'd never seen anything like that before. The technology of those people was first class and pleasing to the eye. There was something that we saw that was odd about these people – we never saw them eating or drinking anything. In form, they were exactly like us. We did see some beings that looked sort of fiery from afar, but when close, normal.

They eventually took the headgear off us, and that was a great relief. The rooms we were in were well decorated. Lots of crystal panelling. I haven't seen anything on Earth to compare with this. Fantastic!

Inside Heidi's room, I said to her, "Have you noticed that so far we've not been hungry or thirsty? That is weird. We probably have become like these people."

Heidi said, "Don't..." looking at me seriously.

"Don't *what?*"

"I know what's inside your mind. and what you're think-ing."

"This one is too big," I told her. "I will not attempt to take it."

"It is far greater and more complicated than the one you took from the artificial planet. This is a mother ship and it is made not to land on a planet. It carries other ships."

Antera at this time was fighting hard against Creslotan. Not many of its ships had been destroyed. Antera, at the same time was transferring the occupants of Earth to their own planet.

On the mother ship belonging to Creslotan, I was really thinking about taking their ship away, but as Heidi said, it was too dangerous, and I remembered the officials on Earth weren't pleased about what I had done, taking the ship away from the artificial planet. I changed my mind. But I knew Heidi and I had the power to change to light and disappear. The people on Creslotan really had no idea what we were capable of.

A few days later, we were in a place which to them was the house of justice. What was strange here, was that the whole system was controlled by robots. I could have burst out laughing, but this was serious business. We were found guilty, taken off the mother ship, onto a small craft, and away to the planet of prisoners.

*

There were about 20 of us all with the headgear on. There was no problem communicating,

The craft we were in came down on a very small planet, reddish-brown with not a tree in sight, but in the distance, a complex of glassy buildings, crystal like. No one could get away from this planet unless they had a craft, and to get one, wasn't easy.

The corridors inside this complex were very large where

people could walk side by side. It was all single rooms when we got there. Just a bed, and a small communication system. I had no plans to definitely stay here for long.

Heidi and I would just disappear before the week was out. We would go back by light to where we came from. I was thinking, why do they need beds here? Do robots sleep? And the other humans? Maybe it is something they cannot get rid of.

8

PEACE TREATY

The crystal fields are amazing, all the beautiful glistening colours. After one month working in those fields, prisoners will be taken back, especially those who behave themselves. Heidi and I were in the craft with 5 others ready to depart. Heidi had said to me, she didn't like the way the pilot robot was behaving. And she was right. There was something wrong.

The craft came much too near to a super galaxy which had a massive black hole with a very high gravitational pull. It was Heidi who rushed to the pilot area from where she was sitting, pushing the robot guard aside, and got the pilot robot in a safe position, before it collapsed. The robot guard immediately sensed what was happening, and did not try to prevent Heidi from doing what she had to do.

There was something not working correctly with his programme chip, and Heidi began to sort the problem out. It was at this time that we learned that Creslotan and Antera were making a peace treaty. That to us was great news.

The craft had not been switched over to automatic pilot, so that made it harder to control if anything went wrong. We went off course to avoid a shower of meteorites – these are the stony ones. While Heidi was trying to fix the robot, I tried to set the craft on light mode, but nothing happened. I called up the master computer for help. At that same time, the craft went spiralling down towards the black hole which was in the centre of the galaxy we were passing by. This was something I didn't want to happen, but here we are experiencing it. If we get into that black hole, we're not going to get back out. Even if the craft was in the light mode, that was no good. Not even light can escape the black hole. To do that, the craft has to be travelling faster than the speed of light, and still no one knows what will happen.

Down and down we went, the craft coming closer and closer to the black hole. There's one thing I know that we shouldn't do, and that is to cross the event horizon. Time acts weird when we get around to the event horizon. It slows down. My memory tickled me, and I brought the super computer in. The next thing I know we were moving away from the black hole.

Everyone on the craft was okay. They could see on the screens what was taking place. We were now well away from danger. Heidi had already sorted the robot pilot out, and it was now able to take over control.

The craft moved away from the black hole, and we saw clearly the photon ring spinning with a yellow-red-bluish light. I was so glad we got away from there. It was an awful place to be.

We were now well away from the black hole. On the big screen, we saw some dark patches. The computer said they were gases and dust travelling at a tremendous speed.

*

There was now total peace between Creslotan and Antera, and we were set free as soon as we got back. Heidi and I were ready to depart from Creslotan, not with any craft, but with our own means of transport - light.

I was thinking as I looked at Heidi. Then I said to her, "Are you ready?" She answered "Yes," and we began to prepare for departing.

The End.

About The Author

John Gumbs grew up on St. Christopher, an island in the West Indies. He came to England as a young man, where he worked on the Nottingham railways as a cleaner and fireman. Later, he joined the British army and got the rank of Corporal. It was in the army where he became interested in writing.

He thinks a lot about life.

Latest by John Gumbs

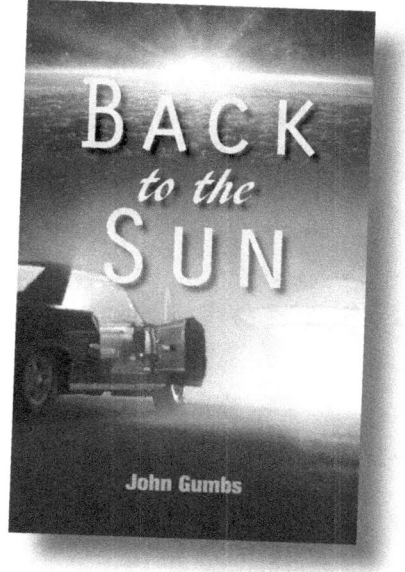

ISBN: 978-1-78792-027-9

Three spacecraft land on Earth, their mission: to find the future.

Also by John Gumbs

Side By Side 978-1-78222-845-5
Jehanne 978-1-78222-571-3
The Trial and Burning of Jehanne 978-1-78222-609-3
Aitch H 978-1-78222-628-4
Jay G 978-1-78222-656-7
Heidi 978-1-78222-682-6
Sheila 978-1-78222-729-8
Just Mates 978-1-78222-751-9
Jay G, Assignment to the Netherlands 978-1-78222-782-3
Jeremy Meets Abigail 9781787920100

www.ingramcontent.com/pod-product-compliance
Lightning Source LLC
Chambersburg PA
CBHW071352130626
46556CB00005B/2154